Fun Home

Music by
Jeanine Tesori

Book and Lyrics by
Lisa Kron

Based on the graphic novel by
Alison Bechdel

A SAMUEL FRENCH ACTING EDITION

SAMUEL
FRENCH
FOUNDED 1830

SAMUELFRENCH.COM
SAMUELFRENCH-LONDON.CO.UK

FOR PRODUCTION ENQUIRIES

UNITED STATES, AUSTRALIA, AND NEW ZEALAND

Info@SamuelFrench.com

1-866-598-8449

UNITED KINGDOM AND IRELAND

Plays@SamuelFrench-London.co.uk

020-7255-4302

Each title is subject to availability from Samuel French, depending upon country of performance. Please be aware that *FUN HOME* may not be licensed by Samuel French in your territory. Professional and amateur producers should contact the nearest Samuel French office or licensing partner to verify availability.

IMPORTANT BILLING AND CREDIT REQUIREMENTS

After securing performance rights to this title, please refer to your licensing agreement for important billing and credit requirements.

PLEASE NOTE:

Originally Produced on Broadway by

Fox Theatricals   Barbara Whitman

Carole Shorenstein Hays

**Tom Casserly   Paula Marie Black   Latitude Link
Terry Schnuck/Jane Lane   The Forstalls**

**Nathan Vernon   Mint Theatricals   Elizabeth Armstrong
Jam Theatricals   Delman Whitney**

and Kristin Caskey & Mike Isaacson

**The world premiere production of *FUN HOME* was produced by
The Public Theater**

Oskar Eustis, Artistic Director; Patrick Willingham, Executive Director

In New York City on October 22nd, 2013

FUN HOME **was developed, in part, at the 2012 Sundance Institute Theatre Lab at White Oak and the 2012 Sundance Institute Theatre Lab at the Sundance Resort.**

sundance
institute

FUN HOME was first produced by the Public Theater (Joseph Papp, Founder; Oskar Eustis, Artistic Director; Patrick Willingham, Executive Director) in New York City on October 22, 2013. The performance was directed by Sam Gold, with sets and costumes by David Zinn, lighting by Ben Stanton, sound by Kai Harada, wigs by Paul Huntley, projections by Jim Findlay and Jeff Sugg, choreography by Danny Mefford, music direction by Chris Fenwick, and orchestrations by John Clancy. The Production Stage Manager was Lisa Dawn Cave. The cast was as follows:

ALISON	Beth Malone
MEDIUM ALISON	Alexandra Socha
SMALL ALISON	Sydney Lucas
BRUCE BECHDEL	Michael Cerveris
HELEN BECHDEL	Judy Kuhn
CHRISTIAN BECHDEL	Griffin Birney
JOHN BECHDEL	Noah Hinsdale
ROY/MARK/PETE/BOBBY JEREMY	Joel Perez
JOAN	Roberta Colindrez

FUN HOME was subsequently produced on Broadway at the Circle in the Square Theatre (Theodore Mann, Artistic Director) on April 19, 2015. The performance was directed by Sam Gold, with sets and costumes by David Zinn, lighting by Ben Stanton, sound by Kai Harada, wigs by Paul Huntley, projections by Jim Findlay and Jeff Sugg, choreography by Danny Mefford, music direction by Chris Fenwick, and orchestrations by John Clancy. The Production Stage Manager was Lisa Dawn Cave. The cast was as follows:

ALISON	Beth Malone
MEDIUM ALISON	Emily Skeggs
SMALL ALISON	Sydney Lucas
BRUCE BECHDEL	Michael Cerveris
HELEN BECHDEL	Judy Kuhn
CHRISTIAN BECHDEL	Oscar Williams
JOHN BECHDEL	Zell Steele Morrow
ROY/MARK/PETE/BOBBY JEREMY	Joel Perez
JOAN	Roberta Colindrez

CHARACTERS

ALISON – *43 years old, a cartoonist*
MEDIUM ALISON – *19 years old, a college freshman*
SMALL ALISON – *around 9 years old*
BRUCE BECHDEL – *Alison's father*
HELEN BECHDEL – *Alison's mother*
CHRISTIAN BECHDEL – *Alison's brother, around 10 years old*
JOHN BECHDEL – *Alison's brother, around 6 years old*
ROY – *a young man Bruce hires to do yard work*
MARK – *a high school junior*
JOAN – *a college student*
PETE – *a mourner*
BOBBY JEREMY *and* **THE SUSAN DEYS** – *imaginary television characters*

The roles of Roy, Mark, Pete, and Bobby Jeremy are performed by the same actor.
The Susan Deys are played by the actors playing Medium Alison and Joan.

SONG LIST

"It All Comes Back (Opening)"
"Welcome To Our House On Maple Avenue"
"Come To The Fun Home"
"Helen's Etude"
"Party Dress"
"Changing My Major"
"Maps"
"Raincoat of Love"
"Pony Girl"
"Ring of Keys"
"Days and Days"
"Telephone Wire"
"Edges of the World"
"Flying Away (Finale)"

FOREWORD

Alison Bechdel's graphic memoir *Fun Home* is so beautifully made and so compelling that it fools us. It feels like a traditional narrative that starts with her childhood and progresses through a linear story; but a closer reading reveals that the book is actually a recursive meditation, circling around and around the four months between when Alison came out to her parents and her father's suicide. And yet the graphic novel makes us feel like we're moving forward in time. This is largely because Alison's depictions of her childhood are so incredibly evocative. But in fact, nothing happens in Alison's childhood, dramatically speaking. Even when her father is arrested, there are no consequences; the family continues on as they were. So why are we so riveted?

It's because we know what this family does not: that they are living a lie and careening toward a tragedy they don't begin to imagine. Our source for this inside information is the narrative voice in the captions that surround every frame, which points out every instance of delusion, denial, hypocrisy, and retroactive irony. The voice is erudite, wry, and aching – the voice of a truth-seeker. It's what makes *Fun Home Fun Home*. We turned that voice into a character and made it the center of our musical. That sounds so wonderfully straightforward and definitive – but it took years to make the whole thing work. By sharing with you some of the thinking that went into our adaptation, we hope we can illuminate some possible paths to successful production.

The difference between novels and plays is stated best (as most things are) by Thornton Wilder, who said, "On the stage it is always now: the personages are standing on that razor-edge, between the past and the future… the words are rising to their lips in immediate spontaneity. A novel is what took place; we hear [the narrator's] voice recounting, recalling events that are past and over." *Fun Home,* the graphic novel, looks back; in *Fun Home,* the musical, we watch characters as they move forward in time.

Theater can't show you a person's inner life; it can only show you behavior. Activities like thinking, feeling, drawing, or remembering can only be shown on a stage if they are externalized. We did this in *Fun Home* by setting three time periods spinning forward. Adult Alison is drawing her memories of the past, and that action calls forth the other two time periods: Alison as a child and Alison as a college student. These scenes from the past flow unbidden and on their own terms, as memories do. And though this is a memory play, it's important to note that the past always understands itself to be the present. Every character in this piece is moving earnestly forward at all times into an unknown and unknowable future. This is even true for adult Alison, for whom looking back is an active journey forward.

It is very important that adult Alison not be misconstrued to be a narrator. She is not talking to the audience. She is not telling us things. She is a character, doggedly pursuing a goal. She is actively combing through her past, determined to piece together a truer version of her father's life than the one she's hung onto since he died. She is working – sketching, drafting, trying out ideas, trying out captions, rejecting them, refining them, and reshaping them as new information comes in. When she begins, this work is an intellectual and artistic quest. She tells us that she "can't abide romantic notions" of the past and is determined to "know what's true / dig deep into who and what and why and when." But the memories Alison excavates draw her, step by step, toward a chasm of long-suppressed emotion, until finally she tumbles over the edge into a fully felt reckoning with the moment of her father's death.

Alison emerges from that reckoning transformed. Led by her imperative to follow the path of truth no matter where it leads, she becomes unmoored from her intellectual safety zone and drawn into a swirling whirl of emotion. Her art requires her to pursue the deepest emotional truth, and by following that path, she is changed.

In writing this musical, we scrupulously wrung out of our scenes the elegiac tone that (so movingly) suffuses the book. It was much harder than it seems like it should be–but whenever we succeeded in situating our scenes in an unfolding present we could feel how much more powerful they became. One of our lighting-bolt moments in this regard came when we realized that we had been writing Medium Alison's coming out with an edge of dread, an overlay of anxiety. But this was because it was recast later in her mind as the catalyst for her father's suicide. But the nineteen-year-old moving forward in time had no such associations. For her, this period was a joyful opening into a wonderful new world.

But it's surprisingly difficult to keep a sense of foreboding or impending sadness from creeping into all sorts of places where it shouldn't be. It's hard to trust that this story will be sad if the characters in it don't know it's going to be sad. But you can trust us when we tell you that the more innocent your characters are of the future, the more the audience will feel the tragedy when it comes. Also, it's tempting to link the scenes in the past to each other, to imply causal connections leading to Bruce's suicide. Don't do that! Each scene from the past must be played for the stakes of that scene itself and should not foreshadow what is to come. It might feel counterintuitive not to draw a narrative arc between these scenes. But if Bruce hadn't killed himself these scenes would never have been collected together in a play. The narrative arc of this musical is located with adult Alison. It's her present-tense assembly of memories that we follow. That, along with the past's innocence of the future, is what makes this musical cohere and come alive.

– Lisa Kron, April 2015

Adult ALISON *enters and crosses to her drawing table. Next to the table, on the floor, is a battered cardboard box. She rummages around inside of it, looking for something to draw. She finds a ring of keys. She arranges it on her table, picks up her pen, and begins to draw.*

Music in.

Enter SMALL ALISON.

SMALL ALISON.
Daddy, hey Daddy, come here, okay? I need you.
What are you doing? I said come here!
You need to do what I tell you to do!
Listen to me.
Daddy!
Come here, hey right here, right now, you're making me mad.
Listen to me.
Listen to me.
Listen to me.
I wanna play airplane
I wanna play airplane
I wanna play airplane
I wanna put my arms out and fly
Like the Red Baron in his Sopwith Camel! No wait–
– like Superman
up in the sky
'Til I can see all of Pennsylvania

        BRUCE *enters with two battered cardboard boxes.*

BRUCE. Hey, gimme a hand.

ALISON. *(Remembering this encounter.)* Right, right, right.

SMALL ALISON. What'd'ja get, Daddy?

9

BRUCE. It's from Clyde Gibbon's barn. What a haul.

He said, "Take what you want," and I said, "You sure, Clyde?" He said, "It's all junk to me," so I said, "Alright, Clyde, alright." Come here. Look.

> *Small Alison looks on as he combs through the box.*

You go to auctions, yard sales, comb the dump and crap, there's crap, there's crap, there's–

> *He pulls out a wrinkled clump of cloth.*

Ah! What's this?

SMALL ALISON. More crap?

BRUCE. *(Rapturously inspecting the wadded fabric.)* No–
Linen
This is...linen
Gorgeous Irish linen
See how I can tell?
Right here, this floating thread, you see?
That's what makes it damask
And the weight, the weight, this drape
And the pattern, crisp and clear
See how it's made from matte and shine
It's tattered here, but all the rest–
How beautiful
How fine
Okay, okay... What else?
Crap...
Crap...
Dead mouse.

SMALL ALISON. Ooh, can I have it?

BRUCE. It's all yours.
What's this?

> *He pulls a grey metal coffee pot from the box.*

Silver
Is this...silver?
Is this junk or silver?

With polish we can tell
I love how tarnish melts away
opening to luster
And the mark, is there a mark?
Yes, this stamp, you see right here?
That's how the craftsman leaves a sign
that he was here and made his work
so beautiful, so fine
This has traveled continents to get here
And crossed an ocean of time
And somehow landed in this box under a layer of grime
I can't abide romantic notions of some vague "long ago"
I want to know what's true,
dig deep into who
and what and why and when,
until now gives way to then

ALISON. Did you ever imagine *I'd* hang on to your stuff, Dad? Me neither. But I guess I always knew that someday I was going to draw you. In cartoons. Yes, Dad, I know you think cartoons are silly, but I draw cartoons. And I need real things to draw from because I don't trust memory.

> **Re: an identical metal coffee pot she's taken from her box.**

But god, this thing is ghastly!
You were so ecstatic when you found it at a yard sale
No, no, wait–
In Mr. Gibbons barn
It all comes back, it all comes back, it all comes back
There's you
And there's me
But now I'm the one who's forty-three
and stuck
I can't find my way through
Just like you
Am I just like you?

ALISON.	BRUCE.
	A sign that he was here
I can't abide romantic notions of	
some vague "long ago"	*and made his work*

ALISON & BRUCE.

I want to know what's true, dig deep into who
and what and why and when,
until now gives way to then

All the characters who will make up this story
(i.e., Alison's memories) swoop in and assemble
the Bechdel house while singing various "la-la's"
as Alison, Small Alison, and Bruce sing:

SMALL ALISON.	BRUCE.	ALISON.
Daddy, hey daddy	*What is true*	*What is true*
come here, okay? I		*Oh–*
need you. What are you	*This has*	
doing? I said come here	*traveled to*	
I wanna play	*get here*	
airplane	*So beautiful*	*I wanna play*
I wanna play		*airplane*
airplane		
I wanna play		
airplane		*I wanna play*
	Beautiful is	*airplane*
	what is true	*What is true*

Bruce lies on the ground and pushes Small Alison
up into a game of airplane. Overjoyed, she laughs
as she flies.

ALISON. Caption: My dad and I were exactly alike.

SMALL ALISON. I see everything!

ALISON. Caption: My dad and I were *nothing* alike.

SMALL ALISON. I'm Superman!

ALISON. My dad and I... My dad and I...

Bruce's attention shifts and he unceremoniously
dumps Small Alison back down to the floor and
exits.

SMALL ALISON. Daddy come back!

ALISON. Caption: Sometimes my father appeared to enjoy having children, but the real object of his affection was his house.

> **JOHN** *and* **CHRISTIAN** *are playing with blocks and trucks.* **HELEN** *is practicing piano. Bruce rushes in with big news.*

BRUCE. I just got a call from Eleanor Bochner! Allegheny Historical Society! She was calling about the house tour!

HELEN. Oh, that's wonderful!

BRUCE. *(Suddenly panicked.)* She's on her way over right now. I'm not sure what to do. This place is turned upside-down... I'm not dressed...

HELEN. *(Taking the situation in hand.)* Go take a shower.

BRUCE. But–

HELEN. Take a shower, get yourself ready.

> ***Bruce exits.***

Kids? An important lady is on her way over here to see the house– Listen to me, please– This is one of those times you need to do what I say quickly and without any shenanigans.

He wants the Hepplewhite suite chairs back in the parlor
Move the GI Joe
It can't be on the floor
He wants the Dresden figurines back in the breakfront
A slinky messes up the period décor
Get the lemon Pledge and dust the–
These should face the same direction
He wants it vacuumed
The surface gleaming
He wants it closer to the door

He wants–
He wants–
He wants–

HELEN. *(cont.)*

> *He wants the brass candelabra set at an angle*
> *The crayons and the glue should go back in the drawer*
> *He wants the bust of Quixote square on the mantel*
> *Sweep that lint away, it's what a broom is for*
> *Gently wipe the eucalyptus*
> *Polish up the crystal prisms*
> *When he comes down here*
> *He wants it ready*
> *We've got to get it done before–*
>
> *He wants–*
> *He wants–*
> *He wants–*

BRUCE. *(Yelling from offstage.)* Where's my bronzing stick!

HELEN. It's in the–

> ***Door slam.***

ALISON.

> *Welcome to our house on Maple Avenue*
> *See how we polish and we shine*
> *We rearrange and realign*
> *Everything is balanced and serene*
> *Like chaos never happens if it's never seen*

ALISON & HELEN.

> *Ev'ry need we anticipate and fill*
> *And still–*

HELEN & SMALL ALISON.

> *He wants the real feather duster used on the bookcase*

HELEN & CHRISTIAN.

> *Find all the books we read and carefully restore*

HELEN & JOHN.

> *He wants them alphabetized by classification*

HELEN.

> *A volume out of place could start a third world war*

HELEN & THE KIDS.

> *That's an inch out of position*
> *Watch it, that's a first edition*

HELEN.

What are we missing?
What have we left out?
When he comes down here what's in store?

HELEN & THE KIDS.

He wants–
He wants–
He wants–

> **Bruce re-enters in a suit and tie and inspects the**
> **now tidy house.**

HELEN, CHRISTIAN,   **BRUCE.**   **ALISON & SMALL**
JOHN.   **ALISON.**

Welcome
to our house on   *Welcome*
Maple Avenue   *to our house on*
                                                 Maple Avenue

See how
we polish and we   *See how*
shine   *we polish and we*
                                                 shine

We rearrange
and realign   *We rearrange*
                                                 and realign

Every-
thing is   *Every-*
balanced   *thing is*   *Every-*
and serene   *balanced*   *thing is*
                        and serene   *balanced*
                                                 and serene

Like
chaos never   *Like*
happens if it's   *chaos never*   *Like*
never seen   *happens if it's*   *chaos never*
                        never seen   *happens if it's*
                                                 never seen

WHOLE FAMILY.

We're a typical family quintet

HELEN.

And yet–

> ***Bruce regards himself in a mirror.***

BRUCE.

Not too bad, if I say so myself
I might still break a heart or two

> *(Sudden burst of agitation:)*

Sometimes the fire burns so hot
I don't know what I'll do.

> *(Back to the mirror.)*

Not too bad, if I say so myself

BRUCE & ALISON.

Not too bad

> ***Bruce, composed and charming, greets the
> [unseen] Mrs. Bochner.***

FAMILY. *(perky but tense)*   **BRUCE.**

Mrs. Bochner, pleasure to
meet you, come on in!

Deet deet...
> *(Responding to
> her admiring
> words about the
> house.)*

Thank you. Obviously
still a work in progress.
Oh yes, I've done all the
work myself. That's how
we're able to afford the

What is he after?   place. No, no, historic
What are we doing?   restoration is an avocation,

Right foot is tapping   but that's very flattering.
That means he's stewing   I teach English at Beech
Creek High, and the
Stay very still and   Bechdel Funeral Home,
maybe we'll please him   is our family business. So
I'm also a funeral director.
Make one wrong move
and demons will seize him
> *(Re: a piece she's
> noticed.)*

FAMILY. *(cont.)*
  Try hard. What else is
  family for?

ALISON. *(simul. with family:)*
  It all comes back…
  It all comes back…

FAMILY.
  He wants–
  He wants–
  He wants–

BRUCE. *(cont.)*
You have a keen eye! This I found yesterday at the dump. [.] Actually I believe Rococo Revival.
  (Re: her request to
  take a picture.)
Absolutely. Would you like one with the family?
Kids! Mrs. Bochner wants to take a photo.
  (Bruce and the
  family pose for a
  photo.)

    ROY *steps into the house. He's young, handsome, and dressed for yard work.*

ROY. Anybody home?

    The camera FLASHES, capturing Bruce posed with his family, and gazing at the young man.

ALISON. *(Taking in her father's gaze.)*
  He wants more

Caption: My Dad and I both grew up in the same small Pennsylvania town
And he was gay.
And I was gay.
And he killed himself.
And I…became a lesbian cartoonist.

    SHIFT *to* **MEDIUM ALISON** *in her dorm room, drawing.*

MEDIUM ALISON. *(Re: her drawing.)*
  Not too bad, if I say so myself
  This outshines the first one I drew
    (Sudden burst of agitation:)
  I don't know which way's up
  I don't know what I'm supposed to do!

MEDIUM ALISON. *(cont.)*

> *(Back to her drawing.)*

Not too bad
If I say so myself…

> **Phone rings.**

MEDIUM ALISON. Hello?

BRUCE. Yes, I'd like to speak to Alison Bechdel, the college student?

MEDIUM ALISON. Hi Dad.

BRUCE. So? How's it going? How are your classes? How's your dorm? How's the food?

MEDIUM ALISON. I'm…getting used to it.

BRUCE. A little homesick?

MEDIUM ALISON. No, it's not that, it's just…stupid stuff. In Modern Classics today the professor told us that Jake's renewal in Spain in *The Sun Also Rises* is really an allusion to *Jungian rebirth*.

BRUCE. What???

MEDIUM ALISON. I almost screamed that's bullshit!

BRUCE. That's bullshit! Jake's not a *symbol*, he's Hemingway! That book is a roman-a-clef.

MEDIUM ALISON. I know! And at dining yesterday I mentioned that my family runs a funeral home and everyone dropped their forks and stared at me like I was Norman Bates.

BRUCE. Typical.

MEDIUM ALISON. I probably just need to find the right people. There must be some people here who aren't total idiots.

BRUCE. Or maybe not. One surprising thing you learn when you go away to college: people just aren't as smart as you want them to be. Trust your instincts, kid. You don't need to twist yourself in knots trying to impress people who are Not Worthy Of You. Got it?

MEDIUM ALISON. Got it. Thanks, Dad.

BRUCE. Good. Alright, I gotta get over to the Fun Home, I've got a viewing in forty-five minutes.

MEDIUM ALISON. Who died?

BRUCE. One of that big clan of Hofbruners over in Lakeview.

MEDIUM ALISON. Ah. Have fun.

BRUCE. Will do. Hey kiddo– Remember what I said, okay?

MEDIUM ALISON. I will, Dad. Thanks.

> *Bruce exits. Medium Alison opens her journal and writes. Alison reads over her shoulder:*

ALISON. "September 15.

"Just had a good talk with Dad and I feel so much better. (Underline, underline, underline.) I'm going to spend four years reading books and drawing. And that's *fine*. I don't know where I got this insane idea I need to throw myself out into the world."

MEDIUM ALISON. It's not the "world" anyway; it's Oberlin College!

> *Medium Alison exits.*

ALISON. Wow. I had no idea what was coming.

> *SHIFT to the Fun Home. Bruce enters the casket showroom with PETE. He sees a dust rag, a can of Pledge, and a tape recorder on top of a casket and whisks them away.*

BRUCE. So sorry, the kids must have been cleaning in here. This is the one we spoke about. Cherry. Quite popular.

PETE. Alright.

BRUCE. Why don't we take these brochures into the office where you can think it over.

PETE. So you say we won't see any of the bruises? With the I.V.'s she was awful beat up by the end.

BRUCE. No, no, we remove all the signs of trauma. Don't worry, Pete. She'll look very peaceful.

PETE. Thank you. Thanks, Bruce.

BRUCE. Of course. Let's–

Indicating they should move to the office.

PETE. *(Re: the brochures.)* No, I'll, I'll take these home.

BRUCE. Sounds good. Take a look and give me a call later.

(They shake hands.)

Get some rest, Pete.

PETE. Thanks, Bruce.

Bruce sees him out, then:

BRUCE. Kids, get out of there.

(Nothing.)

Now!

Christian and Alison appear from the closed ends of a casket.

Where's John?

John appears as well.

How many times have you been told Do Not Get In the Caskets.

JOHN. We were making a commercial for//the Fun Home.

SMALL ALISON. Shhh!!

CHRISTIAN. We're sorry, Dad.

BRUCE. We've got two bodies. We've got work to do.

SMALL ALISON. My turn to do the directory! Who are they?

BRUCE. *(Handing her the directory letters.)* Muriel Swartz. Dwight Johnson.

SMALL ALISON. Wait– Benny's dad?

CHRISTIAN. Benny's in my class!

SMALL ALISON. What happened?

BRUCE. He fell off a ladder. Broke his neck. Get this cleaned up.

(To himself.)

It's going to be a long night.

John and Christian start to clean. Small Alison begins putting the names onto the directory board.

CHRISTIAN. When you break your neck is it just like *crack* you're instantly dead?

JOHN. Probably his head was hanging from his neck and then he couldn't see, and he couldn't eat or anything and then he died from not eating and running into things.

CHRISTIAN. That's not right.

SMALL ALISON. You guys, we gotta practice the commercial.

> *She fetches the tape recorder.*

JOHN. Yeah, we messed it up before.

> *The kids all try to grab the tape recorder.*

SMALL ALISON. Give it to me.

JOHN. I want it.

CHRISTIAN. My turn!

SMALL ALISON. *(Seeing her dad.)* Shhh!

> *Bruce crosses through, now wearing a gown and a surgical mask. The kids try to look innocent. He notices and shoots them a look but keeps moving through. When they're sure he's gone they return to their game.*

CHRISTIAN. Should we start at the top?

SMALL ALISON. Yeah.

CHRISTIAN. Hold on, should we say Fun Home? We only call it that in the family?

JOHN. Yeah, that's right.

SMALL ALISON. It's our commercial. We can do what we want.

JOHN. That's right too.

CHRISTIAN. I guess.

SMALL ALISON. Come on!

CHRISTIAN. Okay, okay!

JOHN. *(Into a fake megaphone.)* Places everybody!

> *They take their places. Small Alison turns on the tape recorder.*

SMALL ALISON. Fun Home commercial. Take seven million billion thousand.

JOHN.

Your uncle died
You're feeling low
You've got to bury your momma but you don't know where to go
Your papa needs his final rest
You got you got you got to give them the best
Oh–

SMALL ALISON & CHRISTIAN.

Come to the Fun Home

JOHN.

That's the Bechdel Funeral Home, baby

SMALL ALISON & CHRISTIAN.

The Bechdel Fun Home

JOHN.

Next to Baker's Department Store

THREE KIDS. in Beech Creek!

SMALL ALISON & CHRISTIAN.

The Bechdel Fun Home

JOHN.

We take dead bodies ev'ry day of the week so

THREE KIDS.

You've got no reason to roam
Use the Bechdel Funeral Home

What it is, what it is
hoo hoo hoo
What it is, what it is now baby

SMALL ALISON/CHRISTIAN.   **JOHN.**

Sock it to me	
Sock it to me	
Sock it to me	
Sock it to me	
Sock it to me	*Ooh–*
Sock it to me	*Here come da judge*
Sock it to me, baby	*Here come da judge, baby*

CHRISTIAN.

Our caskets

SMALL ALISON & JOHN.

Ooh!

CHRISTIAN.

Are satin lined

SMALL ALISON & JOHN.

Ooh!

CHRISTIAN.

And we got so many models guaranteed to blow your mind
You know our mourners–

THREE KIDS.

So satisfied

CHRISTIAN.

They like, they like, they like

THREE KIDS.

our formaldehyde!

SMALL ALISON. Yeah!

THREE KIDS.

Here at the Fun Home

CHRISTIAN.

That's the Bechdel Funeral Home, baby

THREE KIDS.

Come to the Fun Home

SMALL ALISON.

We got kleenex and your choice of psalm

THREE KIDS.

Stop by the Fun Home
Think of Bechdel when you need to embalm
You've got no reason to roam
Use the Bechdel Funeral Home
What it is, what it is
hoo hoo hoo
What it is, what it is
hoo hoo

CHRISTIAN.

> *Tell 'em what we got*
> *What else have we got, Tito?*
> *What else have we got?*
> *What else have we got? WHAAAA!*

SMALL ALISON.

Smelling salts for if you're queasy!

JOHN.

Folding chairs that open easy!

CHRISTIAN.

These are cool, you know what they are?
Flags with magnets for your car!

JOHN.

These are wire and they hold flowers!

SMALL ALISON.

Here's a sign for the names and the hours!

CHRISTIAN.

Stand right here when you sign the book!

JOHN.

This is called an aneurysm hook! En garde!

THREE KIDS.

> *Come to the Fun Home*
> *Ample parking down the street*
> *Here at the Fun Home*
> *Body prep that can't be beat*
> *You'll like the Fun Home*
> *In our hearse there's a backwards seat!*
> *That's why we made up this poem*
> *We're the Bechdel Funeral Home*
>
> *What it is, what it is*
> *hoo hoo hoo*
> *What it is, what it is now baby*
> *hoo! hoo! hoo!*

> ***Big finish: they fall to the ground like corpses.***

BRUCE. *(Calling from the embalming room.)* Alison.

> ***A beat.***

Alison, would you come here, please?

CHRISTIAN. *(Incredulous.)* Does he want you to go back there?

SMALL ALISON. I– I guess.

CHRISTIAN. Why?

SMALL ALISON. I don't know.

BRUCE. *(Getting cross.)* Alison!

> *Small Alison enters the room where Bruce is at work on a cadaver. She's never seen a dead body before.*

Hand me those scissors on the tray.

> *She hands him the scissors, then waits for him to give her more instructions. But he just keeps working. She has no idea what she's supposed to do.*

SMALL ALISON. Is that all?

BRUCE. What? Oh, yeah.

> *Small Alison leaves the embalming room and fetches her diary. She writes. Alison reads over her shoulder.*

ALISON. "Dad showed me a dead body today."

> *Small Alison mulls over what to write next. Then:*

"Went swimming.
Got a new Hardy Boy book.
Had egg salad for lunch."

> *Small Alison closes her journal and leaves.*

What was that about, Dad? Why did you call me back there? Is that the way your father showed you your first dead body? Was it some Bechdel rite of passage? Or, am I reading too much into this? Maybe you just needed the scissors.

> *SHIFT to a door marked "GAY UNION." Medium Alison reaches for the doorknob then loses her nerve. JOAN breezes past her, casually giving her the lesbian nod.*

JOAN. Hey.

MEDIUM ALISON. What? Oh. Hey.

JOAN. Comin' in?

MEDIUM ALISON. Uh, no. Uh, German Club?

JOAN. Oh. Over there.

MEDIUM ALISON. Thanks. Danke.

> *Joan exits into the Gay Union. Awash in humliation, Medium Alison fervently prays:*

Please god, don't let me be a lesbian. Please don't let me be a homosexual.

> *(Hit by a fresh wave of humiliation.)*

Oh my god, *Danke???*

> *SHIFT to the yard where Bruce enters with a sapling and the three kids, conscripted as free labor, trailing behind.*

BRUCE. If we're careful this should bloom in a couple weeks.

> *(To Christian.)*

Hold this.

> *(To John.)*

Gimme that shovel.

> *(To Small Alison.)*

Where's the peat moss?

SMALL ALISON. This bush came from someone else's yard. That's illegal.

BRUCE. No one's lived in that house for five years, nobody's going to miss it.

SMALL ALISON. Fine.

> *She brings him the peat moss. He pours it around the base and pats it down.*

CHRISTIAN. Mom's back from play practice!

> *Helen enters, carrying bags from her rehearsal.*

SMALL ALISON. *(Pulling a bag from Helen's arms.)* Are these your costumes?

HELEN. They are.

JOHN. I wanna see!

CHRISTIAN. Me too!

The kids pull period dresses out of the bags.

HELEN. Careful, careful!

ROY. *(Entering.)* Hey, everybody. Que pasa?

The three kids sidle up to him, shy but thrilled to see him.

SMALL ALISON. Hi Roy.

CHRISTIAN. Hey Roy, what's goin' on?

ROY. *(To John.)* Hey, you look like a guy I met the other day. Are you that same guy? I know what he looked like upside down.

He picks John up and turns him upside down as all three kids laugh and squeal with delight.

HELEN. Hello. I'm Helen Bechdel.

ROY. *(Putting John down to shake her hand.)* Ah, Mrs. Bechdel, yeah, I'm Roy– sorry, I know who you are, my aunt and uncle talk about you all the time, they see your plays, they're crazy about you. They're always saying you're so much better than Irma Hornbacher.

HELEN. *(Blushing.)* Oh. No, Irma's wonderful.

BRUCE. Come on, you're in a different class!

(To Roy.)

I've seen a lot of New York theater, even by those standards she's exceptional.

As he says this, he puts his hand on her shoulder in a gesture that only he and Helen notice is awkward.

SMALL ALISON. Our mom's in a play called Mrs. Warner and the Professor!

HELEN. *Mrs. Warren's Profession.*

SMALL ALISON. She studied in New York with Uta Hagen. Do you know who that is?

ROY. I don't even know what you just said.

BRUCE. Wanna get started?

ROY. Sure. Whatever you want. Lemme get my tools.

BRUCE. 'kay

> *Roy heads out to his car, with the three chattering kids clinging to him.*

SMALL ALISON. Hey Roy, did you see *Herbie Rides Again*?

CHRISTIAN. Oh, yeah! It's the best movie.

JOHN. Herbie is a car!

ROY I didn't see it.

JOHN. *The Love Bug*? You didn't see *The Love Bug*?

> *When they're gone, Helen asks lightly:*

HELEN. Who is that? Why is he here?

BRUCE. I hired him.

HELEN. To do what?

BRUCE. To help me out.

HELEN. Where is he from?

BRUCE. When we went to the lumberyard last week he was there working for Arnie. Kid has a truck, he does hauling. Arnie said he did a good job and he was looking for more work.

HELEN. Oh, so he's just hauling.

BRUCE. Hauling. Other things. I don't know.

HELEN. Oh. So... You're thinking he's going to be working here, at the house?

BRUCE. What difference does it make?

HELEN. I– I– I just–

BRUCE. Arnie recommended him, okay?

HELEN. Okay. I'm just, I'm trying to get a sense // of–

BRUCE. Chrissakes! I know him. He was my student a few years back. Okay? What, do you think I'm bringing some bum around? Is that the bug up your ass? Christ.

The chattering group returns.

JOHN. You know something else about the movie that's funny? It's that the car is called the love bug. // It's a car, but they call it a bug. Even though it's a car.

BRUCE. *(Monster-charging the kids.)* Raaahr!

The kids laugh and scream.

Okay, that's enough. Come on, Roy, let's go inside. I'll show you that wallpaper.

JOHN.	CHRISTIAN.	SMALL ALISON.
Aw!	No, come on!	But dad!

BRUCE. Enough!

(To Roy.)

Bunch of little monsters.

Bruce and Roy leave. Helen watches them go.

CHRISTIAN. Mom, can we watch TV?

HELEN. Sure.

SHIFT to Roy and Bruce entering the library. Helen at her piano. The kids watch TV.

ALISON.

I want to know what's true,
dig deep into who
and what and why and when,
until now gives way to then…

ROY. Whoa. Nice room.

BRUCE. So this is the wallpaper. William Morris. The real deal. God, it's gorgeous.

ROY. You read all these books?

BRUCE. Working on it.

ROY. That is not something I can imagine.

BRUCE. Yes, I remember from class you're not much of a reader.

ROY. Nope. Read some good books in your class, though.

BRUCE. My job is to make it interesting.

Helen begins practicing an étude.

ALISON. *(Re: Bruce and Roy.)* It's like a 1950s lesbian pulp novel. "Their tawdry love could only flourish in the shadows."

Small Alison wanders away from the TV to talk to her mom.

SMALL ALISON. I like Roy. He's funny.

Alison's attention shifts to these two.

HELEN. Alison find something to do. I'm practicing.

SMALL ALISON. *(Peering at Helen's sheet music.)* Did Chop-In write Chop Sticks?

HELEN. It's Sho-PAHN. Alison stop bothering me.

Small Alison rejoins her brothers at the TV.

BRUCE. Sit down. Take a load off.

Alison's attention shifts back to her dad and Roy.

ROY. I been working, I'm disgusting. Don't wanna sweat all over your nice stuff.

BRUCE. What are you talking about, it's *furniture* for chrissakes. Go ahead. Stretch out if you want.

Roy stretches out on the chaise.

ROY. This place is like a museum.

(Noticing a carafe.)

What's that stuff?

BRUCE. Sherry. Want some?

ROY. Is it good?

BRUCE. Yeah.

ROY. Okay, sure.

Bruce pours them both a glass.

I remember this house before you moved in. We used to ride our bikes over here when we were kids. You've done a shit-load of work.

BRUCE. I did. By myself, most of it.

ROY. You must be in good shape, old man.

BRUCE.

Not too bad if I say so myself
I might still break a heart or two
You'd be surprised at what a guy my age knows how to do

He brings the sherry to Roy.

Want it?

ROY. Yeah.

BRUCE. *(Holding the sherry back.)* Unbutton your shirt.

ROY. Is that your wife playing the piano?

BRUCE. Don't worry about her.

Roy considers, decides, why the hell not, and unbuttons his shirt. Bruce gives him the sherry.

HELEN. *(At the piano.)*

La la la la...

Helen stops playing. She stands. Then sits, and resumes playing.

Maybe not right now
Maybe not right now

HELEN.	**BRUCE.**
La la la...	*I want, I want, I want–*
	I–
	I–

ROY.

I know this type
this type of married guy
I could just give him the slip but why
It's not a big deal
I know he wants me

HELEN.	ROY.	BRUCE.	KIDS.
I want	*I know this type*	*I –*	*ba ba ba ba*
I want			
	this type of	*might still*	
I want	*married guy*		*ba ba ba ba*
	I could just	*break a*	
I–	*give him the slip but*	*heart*	*ba ba ba ba*
	why It's not a big deal, I know	*or two*	
La la la	*he wants just*	*I want just*	*ba ba ba ba*
Me and him	*Me and him*	*Me and him*	
Me and him	*Me and him*	*Me and him*	
Me and him	*Me and him*	*Me and him*	

SHIFT to:

MEDIUM ALISON. Dear Mom and Dad,

Thanks for the care package. I was running out of granola bars so it came right in the nick of time. They sell a kind here that I swear is made of paste.

> **Joan enters and gives Medium Alison the lesbian nod.**

(Finishing her letter.) Nothing else worth writing home about (Har har) Al.

> *(To Joan.)*

I can draw you some posters.

JOAN. Nah, we need 'em tomorrow night.

MEDIUM ALISON. I'll do it right now.

JOAN. Really?

MEDIUM ALISON. Just some simple drawing, right? Sure.

> **She sits on her bed to sketch.**

So you want it to say…

JOAN. We just need really good "No Nukes" posters.

MEDIUM ALISON. *(Sketching.)* Right, okay, so something like maybe…

JOAN. Oh, that's funny.

> *(Leaning in to look.)*

That's really good.

MEDIUM ALISON. *(Confident of her ability, but flustered by Joan's nearness.)* This? No. This is just quick and stupid.

> **Medium Alison continues to sketch. Joan looks around her room.**

JOAN. Who's this in the photo?

MEDIUM ALISON. My dad.

JOAN. That's your *dad*?

MEDIUM ALISON. Yeah.

JOAN. He looks cool. Did he teach you how to draw cartoons?

MEDIUM ALISON. *(Scoffs.)* Definitely not.

JOAN. Why's that funny?

MEDIUM ALISON. It's not funny, it's just, he's more… I don't know.

> *(Dismissive eyeroll.)*

Refined.

JOAN. What does he do?

MEDIUM ALISON. A bunch of things, actually. He's a house restoration, historical society kind of guy, he's a high-school English teacher, he runs the // local–

JOAN. *(Making a joke.)* Did you get to be in his class?

MEDIUM ALISON. *(Earnest.)* I was, yeah.

JOAN. Really?

MEDIUM ALISON. Yeah.

JOAN. I was joking.

MEDIUM ALISON. Oh. Oh. Yes. What I was going to say is that, everyone in Beech Creek at some point is in my dad's English class, and he's known as a great teacher, so…

JOAN. Oh. Cool.

MEDIUM ALISON. Yeah. He sends me books. We talk about them.

JOAN. He sends you books to read on top of your schoolwork?

MEDIUM ALISON. Yeah.

JOAN. That's a little weird.

ALISON. *(Realizing.)* Is that weird? That's really weird.

MEDIUM ALISON. Why?

JOAN. I don't know. Like, what books?

MEDIUM ALISON. Like…

JOAN. Colette??

MEDIUM ALISON. Yeah.

> ### She hands her a book.

JOAN. Your father sent you *Colette?*

MEDIUM ALISON. Yeah. Why?

JOAN. I don't know. It's just… He's like the opposite of my dad. He's just like sending you lesbian books?

MEDIUM ALISON. No! I mean, yes, I guess Colette was a lesbian but–

JOAN. Oh, she was.

MEDIUM ALISON. Okay, but he sent it to me because he thought I'd be interested in the whole Paris… Arts… Bohemian… Scene.

JOAN. Yeah but he didn't send you a book about Toulouse-Latrec, he sent you Colette. I think it's amazing that he's cool with you being a dyke.

MEDIUM ALISON. What? I don't think so.

JOAN. Oh, he's not?

MEDIUM ALISON. No. I don't know. Can we talk about something else?

JOAN. Sure. Why?

MEDIUM ALISON. Because– I have no idea how my parents feel about– I just figured it out myself.

JOAN. Oh.

MEDIUM ALISON. About two weeks ago.

JOAN. Huh. With who?

MEDIUM ALISON. With who what?

ALISON. *(A wave of retroactive humiliation.)* Oh god.

JOAN. Who were you with?

MEDIUM ALISON. *(Clueless, then getting it.)* Nobody. *Nobody!* Oh my god, I'm so embarrassed.

ALISON. *(Fresh wave of retroactive humiliation.)* Oh god.

MEDIUM ALISON. I was in a bookstore.

JOAN. In a bookstore? Nice.

MEDIUM ALISON. *(Clueless, then getting it.)* What? *NO!* Two weeks ago I was downtown and I wandered into the bookstore, I was just browsing around and I picked up this book–

JOAN. Ah, *Word is Out.*

MEDIUM ALISON. And I was like, Oh, interviews. This looks interesting. And then I was like, These people are all–

> *(Suddenly worried she doesn't know the right word.)*

Uh…

JOAN. Gay?

MEDIUM ALISON. Gay. Yes. And *then* I was like, "Oh my god! *I'm*

MEDIUM ALISON.	**JOAN.**
a lesb–	a dyke

MEDIUM ALISON. Yes. A dyke. Yes. And I totally flipped out and shoved the book back onto the shelf and I left. And then I came back the next day and bought the book. And then I came back the next day bought all the other books in that section. And then I made myself go to the meeting at the Gay Union. And then, and then, it's now. Hi.

JOAN. Hello.

> *(A beat. Then, re: Word is Out.)*

That's a powerful book.

MEDIUM ALISON. It is.

> *Joan considers kissing her. Medium Alison wonders whether she's about to be kissed.*

JOAN. So. I should probably go.

MEDIUM ALISON. 'kay.

JOAN. So… Will I see you at the Union meeting tomorrow afternoon?

MEDIUM ALISON. Yeah I'll be, uh, yeah, I will come to the meeting. I'll bring these posters. Finish 'em up.

JOAN. Cool. I'll see you then. Bye, Alison.

MEDIUM ALISON. Bye, Joan.

> *Joan exits. Medium Alison collapses, face-down, onto the bed. Alison crumples as well.*

> *SHIFT to Bruce, dressed in a suit, holding a pair of patent-leather Mary Janes as Small Alison, tears around in an awkwardly fitting party dress she's covered up with a boy's t-shirt and sneakers.*

BRUCE. Oh no you don't. T-shirt off.

> *Small Alison grudgingly takes off the t-shirt. Bruce re-ties the sash.*

Look, you've messed this up already. Where's your barrette?

> *Small Alison hands it over. He puts it in her hair.*

SMALL ALISON. Ow!

BRUCE. Sneakers.

SMALL ALISON. Why??

BRUCE. Because you're going to a party.

> *(Holding out the Mary Janes.)*

Here.

SMALL ALISON. I don't want to wear those.

BRUCE. Tough titty.

SMALL ALISON.

I despise this dress.
What's the matter with boy's shirts and pants?

BRUCE. You're a girl.

SMALL ALISON.

This dress makes me feel like a clown.

I hate it!

BRUCE. That's enough. We're late.

SMALL ALISON. You're wearing a girl color.

> *An eye-blink of rage which he channels into ultra-calm rationality.*

BRUCE. Every other girl at this party is going to be wearing her prettiest dress and you want to put on... What? What? Your jean jacket? Trousers? S'alright with me. You understand you'll be the *only* girl there not wearing a dress, right? Is that what you want? You want everyone talking about you behind your back. S'alright with me, change your clothes. Well? Go ahead. You gonna change?

SMALL ALISON.

Maybe not right now.
Maybe not right now.

MEDIUM ALISON. Dear Mom and Dad–

BRUCE. *(Exiting.)* Good.

MEDIUM ALISON.	**SMALL ALISON.**
– I'm trying to tell you something and I'm having a hard time because it's kind of a big deal. It's not that big of a deal! It might be a big deal! I don't know! *I want– I want– I want– I–* – am a lesbian! Dear Mom and Dad, I am a lesbian.	*La la la la...*

> *Joan enters.*

JOAN. Hey.

MEDIUM ALISON. I did it!

JOAN. Did what?

MEDIUM ALISON. I told my parents.

JOAN. Told them what?

MEDIUM ALISON. That I'm a lesbian.

JOAN. Oh. How are they taking it? What do they say?

MEDIUM ALISON. Oh. Nothing. I just put it in the mailbox just now.

JOAN. Oh.

MEDIUM ALISON. But I feel so...*tough!* So sure of myself. So many things, oh my god, so many things just suddenly make so much sense!

JOAN. Like, oh, that's why I was in love with my first grade teacher!

MEDIUM ALISON. *(Huge revelation.)* That *is* why I was in love with my first grade teacher.

JOAN. *(Shaking her hand.)* Welcome, my friend. Welcome to the club.

MEDIUM ALISON. *(Shaking back.)* Thank you. Thank you very much.

JOAN. Okay! Okay, new lesbian, we are going to the party at the Women's Collective tonight.

> ***Confidence instantly vaporized.***

MEDIUM ALISON. Oh. Uh...

JOAN. What?

MEDIUM ALISON. Oh, uh. It's just– I just have a lot of work.

JOAN. No you don't.

MEDIUM ALISON. Yes I do.

JOAN. What's going on?

MEDIUM ALISON. Nothing.

JOAN. What?

MEDIUM ALISON. I don't know if I fit in.

JOAN. With who?

MEDIUM ALISON. The lesbians. The real lesbians. You know what I mean. They're political and socially conscious and– Real lesbians. Look the only thing I really know about myself is that I'm asexual. I am. I'm not attracted to men but that doesn't necessarily mean I'm attracted to women.

> *Joan kisses her. Medium Alison is flummoxed for a beat, then lunges at Joan in an uncontrollable and totally inexperienced onslaught of pent up lust.*

JOAN. Okay.

> *Medium Alison leaps on her again and they tumble into bed.*

ALISON. *(HUGE wave of retroactive humiliation.)* Oh my god it's so embarrassing.

> *She picks up Medium Alison's journal and reads:*

"Went to a meeting the Gay Union tonight. I was petrified. A lot of political talk. Almost too much, but ultimately a reasonable amount."
What does that mean?
"I signed up to help organize a 'Take Back the Night March.' I don't know why I did it. I don't know what that is." Oh my god.

MEDIUM ALISON.
> *What happened last night?*
> *Are you really here?*
> *Joan Joan Joan Joan Joan*
> *Hi Joan Don't wake up, Joan*
> *Oh my god last night*
> *Oh my god Oh my god Oh my god Oh my god last night*
> *I got so excited*
> *I was too enthusiastic*
> *Thank you for not laughing*
> *Well you laughed a little bit*
> *at one point when I was touching you*
> *and said I might lose consciousness*

MEDIUM ALISON. *(cont.)*

which you said was adorable
and I just have to trust that you don't think I am an idiot
or some kind of an animal
I never lost control
due to overwhelming lust
But I must say that I'm

Changing my major to Joan
I'm changing my major to sex with Joan
I'm changing my major to sex with Joan
with a minor in kissing Joan
Foreign study to Joan's inner thighs
A seminar on Joan's ass in her Levis
And Joan's crazy brown eyes

Joan, I feel like Hercules
Oh god that sounds ridiculous
Just keep on sleeping through this
and I'll work on calming down
so by the time you've woken up
I'll be cool I'll be collected
and I'll have found some dignity
but who needs dignity?
'cause this is so much better
I'm radiating happiness
Will you stay here with me
for the rest of the semester?
We won't need any food
We'll live on sex alone
Sex with Joan!

I am writing a thesis on Joan!
It's a cutting edge field and my mind is blown
I will gladly stay up ev'ry night to hone
My compulsory skills with Joan
I will study my way down her spine
Familiarize myself with her well-made outline
While she researches mine!

I don't know who I am
I've become someone new

Nothing I just did
is anything I would do
Overnight everything changed, I am not prepared
I'm dizzy I'm nauseous I'm shaky I'm scared
Am I falling into nothingness
or flying into something so sublime?
I don't know!
But I'm

Changing my major to Joan
I thought all my life I'd be all alone
But that was before I was lying prone
in this dorm room bed with Joan
Look, she drooled on the pillow– so sweet
All sweaty and tangled-up in my bed sheet
And my heart feels...
Complete

Let's never leave this room
How 'bout we stay here 'til finals
I'll go to school forever
I'll take out a dementedly huge high-interest loan
'Cause I'm changing
my major
to Joan

SHIFT to:

ALISON. Caption: I leapt out of the closet– and four months later my father killed himself by stepping in front of a truck.

> ***Bruce sits in his chair, reading a book. Alison watches him, incredulous.***

While I was at college, exploding into my new life, you...were sitting here reading a book.

> ***Helen and Small Alison are working in another room: Helen is grading papers, Small Alison is working on a school project.***

SMALL ALISON. Mom, I have a question.

HELEN. What?

SMALL ALISON. What was the name of that street you lived on in New York?

HELEN. Bleecker?

SMALL ALISON. Yeah, good.

> *(She dives back into her drawing, then:)*

Mom, I have a question.

HELEN. What?

SMALL ALISON. When Dad was in the Army in Germany what color was your house?

HELEN. Well, it was an apartment, not a house. And– I don't remember what color it was.

SMALL ALISON. Alright something else about what it looked like then.

HELEN. Uh... Well, we had a balcony, we had a lovely balcony and in the mornings friends of ours would come over and we'd sit there and talk and have breakfast.

SMALL ALISON. Okay, where did you live after that?

HELEN. Here. Your grandfather died while we were there, so we came back.

SMALL ALISON. Oh yeah, 'cause Daddy had to run the Fun Home.

HELEN. Yes.

SMALL ALISON. *(On a new track.)* Oh, I know!

> **Taking her drawing, she finds her dad.**

Daddy, you saw the Leaning Tower of Pisa one time, right?

BRUCE. I did.

> *(Re: her drawing.)*

What's that?

SMALL ALISON. *(Excited to show him.)* In school we're learning maps and globes, and Miss Windsor said draw a map of all places people in our family have been to.

BRUCE. Aha.

SMALL ALISON. They're for showing tomorrow in class.

BRUCE. What's this?

SMALL ALISON. *(Bursting with pride.)* Okay, so: This is a keystone because Pennsylvania is the Keystone state.

BRUCE. This square?

SMALL ALISON. That's Beech Creek, see? That's the bridge, that's the ford, that's the creek, school, the Fun Home, our house, Aunt Jane and Uncle Randy's house–

> *Bruce points.*

That's Germany!

> *(Getting an idea.)*

Ooh, I know.

> *She draws in a new part.*

John, Christian, me. See? Floating in bubbles because we're not born yet–

BRUCE. Okay, that's interesting but let me show you how you can make it better. This is visually confusing; you've got about ten different drawings so you can't really see any of them. Pick one.

SMALL ALISON. But this is a cartoon and in a cartoon there's all different parts.

BRUCE. But we can make it better than a cartoon.

SMALL ALISON. I like cartoons.

BRUCE. Sure, cartoons are fun but I'm showing you here how to do something substantial and beautiful. Listen to me, you have the potential to become a real artist. Do you know that? You do. But that means you have to learn the craft, you have to study the rules. Let's talk about composition. You've got too much going on here. Pick one area.

SMALL ALISON. The Keystone State.

BRUCE. That's too much. Watch this.

> *He takes her pad and starts a new drawing.*

I'm going to draw our mountains. See that? How I'm shading them? That gives them dimension.

BRUCE. *(cont.)*
> *Make this part look rugged...*
> *Hm mm*
> *Allegheny Plateau...*
> *This dark shaded stripe bum bum bum is the front*
> *Paint the long ridges and valleys below*
> *Hm mm*

SMALL ALISON. I want the whole state.

BRUCE. *(Cross.)* I'm explaining to you that you can't do that.

SMALL ALISON. Let me try.

BRUCE. Alison, this is the way it should look.

SMALL ALISON. But I liked the way mine was.

BRUCE. *(Losing his temper.)* But you cannot do it like that unless you want to ruin it. I am trying to teach you something important.

HELEN. *(Coming in from the other room.)* Bruce, it doesn't matter. It's a drawing.

BRUCE. What do you mean it doesn't matter? She's taking it to school. She's showing it in class. You know what, never mind. You want to take a half-baked mess to school, you want to embarrass yourself like that it's fine with me. Do what you want.

SMALL ALISON. *(Holding the drawing out to him.)* No, I like the one you did, Daddy.

> ***Alison takes the drawing from Small Alison's outstretched hand and studies it.***

ALISON.
> *Make this part look rugged...*
> *Mm mm*
> *Allegheny Plateau...*
> *This dark shaded stripe bum bum bum is the front*
> *Paint the long ridges and valleys below*
> *Mm mm*
> *Our town is this...dot.*

> ***She begins to draw her own version of this map:***

> *Quick dashes mark the property ends*
> *Beech Creek, a rope that turns and bends*

Little squares for houses strung along roads
The land transfigured into topographic codes

Maps show you what is simple and true
Try laying out a bird's eye view
Not what he told you, just what you see
What do you know that's not your dad's mythology?

Dad was born on this farm
Here's our house
Here's the spot where he died
I can draw a circle
His whole life fits inside

Four miles from our door
I-80 ran from shore to shore
On its way from the Castro to Christopher Street
The road not taken, just four miles from our door

You were born on this farm
Here's our house
Here's the spot where you died
I can draw a circle
I can draw a circle
You lived your life inside

SHIFT to Bruce in his car. He's pulled over to talk to MARK.

BRUCE. Hey, Mark. Is that you?

MARK. Oh. Hey, Mr. Bechdel.

BRUCE. You wanna lift?

MARK. I'm not goin' far.

BRUCE. I'm happy to give you a ride. Let me move these groceries. Get in.

Mark gets in. They drive.

So, Mark. How's your summer? You got a job?

MARK. Yeah, working in the stockroom at Cosgrove's.

BRUCE. Good. Staying on track. That's great. Wanna beer?

MARK. I don't… I don't think I better.

BRUCE. It's okay. There's some in the bag.

*Mark takes a beer, little nervous but it's also kind
of fun. They drive for a beat.*

MARK. Oh, uh, my house is down that way, Mr. Bechdel.

BRUCE. I know. I just like getting the chance to know you a
little better. You got yourself a girl?

MARK. Nah.

BRUCE. Saving for college? You a senior?

MARK. Junior.

BRUCE. Ah, right.

SHIFT to:

MEDIUM ALISON. Dear Mom and Dad,
I assume you got my letter. I haven't heard from you.
I'd really love some sort of response.

**SHIFT to Small Alison watching a Partridge
Family-esque show on TV:**

SOUND FROM THE TV.
(A kid's voice:)

I guess you're not too bad…for a manager.

(Canned laughter. A man's voice:)

And I guess you kids aren't so bad either– even if you *do*
wear chicken feathers.

(Canned laughter, then a young man's voice:)

A-one, a-two, a-one two three four–

(Sound of family singing-group:)

Ba Ba Ba Ba….
Everything's alright, babe
When we're together
When we're together
'Cause you are like a raincoat
Made out of love…

Bruce enters, and snaps off the TV.

BRUCE. God, it's inane.

SMALL ALISON. I was watching it!

BRUCE. That show's awful.

SMALL ALISON. It's the best show! It's about a family that–

BRUCE. I know what it's about. Read a book.

> *He stands in front of a mirror straightening his tie.*

SMALL ALISON. How come you're wearing a suit?

BRUCE. I'm going to Danville.

SMALL ALISON. *(Making a joke, twirling her finger by the side of her head.)* Are you going to the mental hospital?

BRUCE. *(Slight beat.)* Yes.

SMALL ALISON. *(Taken aback.)* You *are?*

BRUCE. I have to see a psychiatrist.

SMALL ALISON. How come?

BRUCE. Because I do dumb dangerous things. Because I'm bad. Not good like you.

ALISON. Actually it's because you were arrested, Dad. On a charge of "furnishing a malt beverage to a minor," which I believe is what they call a euphemism.

> *Bruce exits leaving Small Alison to digest this information. Helen enters on her way to do the laundry.*

SMALL ALISON. Daddy said he's going to Danville.

HELEN. *(Taken aback that Small Alison was told this.)* Oh.

SMALL ALISON. He said he's going to see a psychiatrist?

HELEN. He is.

SMALL ALISON. How come?

HELEN. The…um… A judge said he had to go. It's been very…complicated. We thought we might have to move, and then–

SMALL ALISON. Move?? Where would we go??

HELEN. We don't have to move. The judge said your dad could– could– see someone instead. I can't explain it any better. You don't need to worry. Everything's going to be fine.

Helen leaves. Small Alison is again left alone.

ALISON. Oh yes, it's all gonna be just fine.

(*Speaking aloud the words she's drawing:*)

Slam. Crash.

We hear an offstage fight. Small Alison hears it too. Alison continues to draw.

BRUCE.	ALISON.
Who fucking left these here? I just varnished this table!	(*Murmuring words as she writes them.*)

HELEN.

Bruce–	…varnished

(*Sound of him tearing pages out of the books.*)

Bruce, what are you doing! Those are library books!! // Stop it!	…library…books

BRUCE.

Take these back to the library you crazy, // stupid bitch!

HELEN.   …stupid

Go! Go! Just go! You're going to be late for your // appointment. Just go.

BRUCE.

Don't fucking tell me what to do!

HELEN.

Bruce if you miss this appointment we are in a lot of trouble. // Do you understand that?	…trouble

BRUCE. Thank you for the lecture. // I can handle my own business!

HELEN. If you're not home for dinner I'm throwing it in
the toilet!

> *Small Alison has shut her eyes and covered her
> ears to block out the fight. Now she starts trying
> to sing over it.*

SMALL ALISON.
*Ba ba ba ba
ba ba ba ba
Ba ba ba ba
ba ba ba ba ba*

THE KIDS, BOBBY JEREMY, THE SUSAN DEYS. *(offstage)*
*Ba ba ba ba
ba ba ba ba
Ba ba ba ba
ba ba ba ba ba*

> *Small Alison's brothers hand her a tambourine.
> Then she turns and sees:* **BOBBY JEREMY** *and his
> backup singers,* **THE SUSAN DEYS***!*

BOBBY JEREMY.
Today I woke up with this feeling that I did not recognize
KIDS & THE SUSAN DEYS.
Strange feeling yeah
BOBBY JEREMY.
Our happy life seemed far away and everything was made of lies
KIDS & THE SUSAN DEYS.
Lies yeah
BOBBY JEREMY.
*The sky was turning dark when baby I looked in your eyes
And that's when I knew*

> *Bruce and Helen join as well. Now they're a
> happy, singing family!*

ALL.
Everything's all right babe,
BOBBY JEREMY.
when we're togethah

FAMILY & THE SUSAN DEYS.

when we're together

BOBBY JEREMY.   **ALL.**

Cuz

you are like a raincoat   *you are like a raincoat*

made out of love

FAMILY & THE SUSAN DEYS.

Keepin' me dry!

ALL.

Magic shield of love

BOBBY JEREMY.

Protecting me from bad weathah

FAMILY & THE SUSAN DEYS.

Rain from the sky

ALL.

You are like a raincoat!

BOBBY JEREMY.

Made out of love

FAMILY & THE SUSAN DEYS.

ba ba ba ba ba ba

ALL.

A raincoat of love love love love love!

Everything's all right babe

BOBBY JEREMY.

When we're togethah

FAMILY & THE SUSAN DEYS.

When we're togethah

ALL.

Cuz you are like a raincoat

BOBBY JEREMY.

made out of love

HELEN & THE KIDS.

Keepin' me dry!

ALL.

Magic shield of love

BOBBY JEREMY.

protecting me from bad weathah

HELEN, KIDS, THE SUSAN DEYS.

Rain from the sky

ALL.

You are like a raincoat!

BOBBY JEREMY.

Made out of love
A raincoat of love

HELEN, BRUCE,   **KIDS.**

THE SUSAN DEYS.

Love love love love love

Love love love love love   *Together Together together*

FAMILY.   **BOBBY JEREMY & THE SUSAN**

DEYS.

Everything's all right babe,   *Ba ba ba, etc.*
when we're togethah
Everything's all right babe,
when we're togethah
Everything's all right babe,
when we're togethah

> **The TV world melts away leaving only Bruce,**
> **singing alone, slightly manic and upbeat. Alison**
> **watches him.**

BRUCE.

Everything's all right
Everything's all right
Everything's all right

ALISON. It's only writing, it's only drawing, I'm
remembering something, that's all.

> **SHIFT to: sounds of loud, whooshing New**
> **York City traffic. Bruce enters a small, shabby**
> **Greenwich Village apartment with Small Alison,**
> **Christian, and John trailing behind, dragging**
> **big shopping bags from their day in the city. As**
> **Bruce heads for the bathroom to wash up, Small**

> *Alison and Christian close front door on John,*
> *who pounds from the other side.*

JOHN. Hey, let me in!

SMALL ALISON. Are you a Land Shark?

> *She and Christian crack up.*

JOHN. *(Pounding, nearly crying.)* Let me in!

CHRISTIAN. Land Shark. You have to say Land Shark.

BRUCE. Kids, let him in.

> *They open the door and John bursts through, and*
> *heads right to his sleeping bag on the floor, where*
> *he quickly falls asleep.*

Don't play in the hall like that. Ellie told us her neighbors don't like it. She won't let us stay here again if you do that.

ALISON. Caption… Caption… Uh… Clueless in New York. In denial in New York. Family Fun in New York. Child neglect in New York. I don't know…

> *Christian and Small Alison look through the*
> *shopping bags. Small Alison pulls out a box of*
> *Li-Lac Chocolates.*

SMALL ALISON. Can I eat one of these chocolates?

BRUCE. No, those are to take home for your mother. Put them back.

> *She takes a huge book out of a Rizzoli bag.*

SMALL ALISON. Can I look at the Baryshnikov book?

BRUCE. Yes but be careful with it.

SMALL ALISON. What's the name of that museum we're going to tomorrow?

BRUCE. The Frick.

SMALL ALISON. Oh yeah.

> *Christian is looking through a Playbill from* **A**
> **Chorus Line.** *He and Small Alison giggle and*
> *whisper about the naughty parts:*

CHRISTIAN. Remember this song?

> *(singing)*
>
> *"Shit Richie, Shit Richie"*

SMALL ALISON. That was so funny. What about the song about the…*tits and ass?*

CHRISTIAN. Oh yeah.

> *(Lots of giggling.)*

BRUCE. Kids, wash up.

> ***Alison focuses her attention on recalling and drawing details from the apartment.***

ALISON. Okay… Sleeping bags. Shopping bags. Window was open. Really hot. Stinky– no, no… *Humectant. "The humectant air."* Something on *"The humectant air."* Good phrase. Okay, good.

BRUCE. Get into bed. It's late.

> ***Small Alison and Christian brush their teeth. There's a big explosion noise outside. A car alarm goes off. John doesn't stir but the other two run to the window. Alison looks as well.***

CHRISTIAN. Whoa! I think somebody blew up that garbage can.

ALISON. *(Remembering.)* Fireworks.

BRUCE. Just homemade fireworks.

CHRISTIAN. There's so many sailor guys.

BRUCE. That's 'cause there's ships here from all over the world.

CHRISTIAN. For the bicentennial?

BRUCE. Yeah.

> *(Getting them settled.)*

Come on. Lay down. Go to sleep. Big day tomorrow.

> ***Alison pulls her attention away from her father and tries to re-focus herself on remembering and drawing things about the apartment.***

ALISON. Oh my sleeping bag, I *loved* that sleeping bag. Kids In Bags. And…*four locks* on the front door. Amazing. Oh yeah. Coat hook with jackets piled like…twenty deep on the one hook. Crazy. Oh yes, that basket with the *Village Voices.*

> *Bruce turns out all the apartment lights and heads for the door. Small Alison sits up.*

SMALL ALISON. Where are you going?

BRUCE. Oh. Just out. Just for a minute. What's a matter, you can't sleep? I'm just running out for a newspaper. I'll be back in a sec. You're going to fall asleep so fast you'll be asleep before I get back.

SMALL ALISON. But where are you going?

BRUCE. I said. I'm going out for a paper. Alright?

> *Small Alison is unconvinced. A beat.*

You want me to sing to you?

> *Small Alison nods and lays down.*

Pony girl ride, ride away
I knew you'd break my heart someday
Some folks get the call to go
Some folks are bound to stay
Oh ride, ride, ride away
Ride, ride, ride away
Ride, ride…

> *He checks. Her eyes are closed. He slips out. At the sound of the lock Small Alison sits upright, staring at the closed apartment door.*

ALISON. Caption: Dad goes out. Dad gets a newspaper. Dad goes…cruising? Dad picks up a hustler? No he didn't. Maybe he did. I don't really know. Who knows?

> *SHIFT to Medium Alison and Joan. Medium Alison is reading a letter. She's agitated, distressed.*

JOAN. What happened?

MEDIUM ALISON. Dad finally responded to my letter.

JOAN. Oh my god. What does he say?

MEDIUM ALISON. *(She reads:)*

"Dear Al,

"Sorry I've been out of touch for a bit. Big week here at Fun Home. Couple of kids from Lock Haven wrapped their car around a tree and I ended up working two eighteen-hour shifts. Bad for my blood pressure. Oh, by the way, we got your letter. Well, kid, talk about a flair for the dramatic."

> *Bruce enters, picking up the letter where she left off. Medium Alison stays in the scene with Joan.*

BRUCE. As far as I see it the good news is, you're human.

MEDIUM ALISON. What does that mean? What else would I be?

BRUCE. Your mother's pretty upset though– not surprisingly, I guess. But I'm of the opinion that everyone should experiment.

MEDIUM ALISON. *(Grossed-out.)* Seriously?

BRUCE. I can't say, though, that I see the point of putting a label on yourself. There have been a few times in my life when I thought about taking a stand, but I'm not a hero. Is that a cop out? Maybe so. It's hard sometimes to tell what is really worth it.

> *He exits.*

MEDIUM ALISON. *(Angry, outraged, hurt.)* God, I just–

JOAN. I'm sorry.

MEDIUM ALISON. The *tone* is what I can't stand. It's so typical. So all-knowing. He has to be the expert. Lots of wisdom and advice about things he doesn't know anything about! I'm gay. Which means I'm not like him, and I've *never* been like him, and he can't deal with that. He still wants to be the…the intellectual, broad-minded, liberal, *bohemian* but he can't pull it off because he can't deal with me, and you know what? He never could. He never could.

> *SHIFT to a diner. Bruce and Small Alison sit at a table. Bruce reads a newspaper.*

BRUCE. I need more coffee. Where's Betty?

SMALL ALISON. She went home. Lorna's on now.

BRUCE. Oh.

(Re: the newspaper.) Huh.

SMALL ALISON. What?

BRUCE. Bill Smoot's running for town council. He didn't mention it at Rotary. Hey. Where's your barrette?

> **Small Alison grudgingly pulls it out of her pocket.**

Put it back in. It keeps the hair out of your eyes.

SMALL ALISON. *(Under her breath as she puts it back in.)* So would a crew cut.

BRUCE. If I see you without it again I'll wale you. Go find Lorna. I need coffee.

> **He goes back to his paper. Small Alison gets up to fetch Lorna but, at the sound of a jingling bell, is stopped in her tracks.**

ALISON. You didn't notice her at first but I saw her the moment she walked in. She was a delivery woman; came in with a handcart full of packages. She was an old-school butch.

SMALL ALISON.

Someone just came in the door
Like no one I ever saw before
I feel–
I feel–
I don't know where you came from
I wish I did, I feel so dumb
I feel–

Your swagger and your bearing
and the just-right clothes you're wearing
Your short hair and your dungarees and your lace up boots
and your keys, oh, your ring of keys

I thought it was supposed to be wrong
but you seem okay with being strong
I want–
You're so–

It's prob'ly conceited to say
but I think we're alike in a certain way
I, um–

Your swagger and your bearing
and the just-right clothes you're wearing
Your short hair and your dungarees and your lace up boots
and your keys, oh, your ring of keys

Do you feel my heart saying hi?
In this whole luncheonette why am I the only one
who sees you're beautiful–
No.
I mean… Handsome

Your swagger and your bearing
And the just-right clothes you're wearing
Your short hair and your dungarees and your lace up boots
And your keys
Oh, your ring of keys

I know you
I know you
I know you

> **Bruce has lowered his paper and is watching Small Alison. Their eyes meet. He returns to his paper.**

> **A phone ring. SHIFT to:**

BRUCE. Hello?

MEDIUM ALISON. Hey, Dad.

BRUCE. Kiddo. How are ya?

MEDIUM ALISON. I got your response to my letter.

BRUCE. Oh. Oh good.

MEDIUM ALISON. It was a little confusing.

BRUCE. Ah. Listen, before I forget, d'ja get the book I sent? The Joyce. *Portrait of the–*

MEDIUM ALISON. Yes, I got it.

BRUCE. You better damn well identify with every page!

MEDIUM ALISON. If you don't want to talk to me about my letter put Mom on the phone.

BRUCE. Well, she's watching something on TV.

MEDIUM ALISON. Would you ask her, please, if she'll talk to me?

BRUCE. Sure.

> ### *Shift to Helen.*

HELEN. Hello?

MEDIUM ALISON. Hi, Mom.

HELEN. How are you? How's your school work?

MEDIUM ALISON. It's…fine.

Are you ever going to talk to me about my letter?

> *(Small beat.)*

HELEN.	MEDIUM ALISON.
I'm– I'm really at odds here. I feel responsible–	
	Mom, you didn't cause this– That's not the way it works
I do feel children should be allowed to make their own mistakes.	
You know that and you know that I don't like parents who meddle, but in this case I'm uniquely qualified to warn you against romanticizing this path. Alison, you probably don't know that on more than one occasion catastrophe has been narrowly averted and it is difficult for me to–	Oh please!
	Catastrophe? Could you be a little more overdramatic?

HELEN. Alison, your father has had affairs with men.

> *(A beat.)*

MEDIUM ALISON. What?

HELEN. I don't know how he hasn't been caught or exposed. There was the thing with Roy.

MEDIUM ALISON. *(Dumbfounded.)* Our yard guy? Our *babysitter???*

HELEN. What do you think he was doing when he went out in the middle of the night, or taking his "trips"? One time he came back with body lice. It's been going on for years. For our whole marriage, actually.

MEDIUM ALISON. Why are you telling me this and not Dad?

HELEN. Your father? Tell the truth? Please.

SHIFT to:

JOAN. No. What? Your *dad???* Oh my god. Are you okay?

MEDIUM ALISON. I'm fine.

JOAN. Are you sure? Do you need to talk about it?

MEDIUM ALISON. No. No, I don't want to talk about it, I don't want to think about it. I want to– I don't know. Let's go see what's happening at the Gay Union.

JOAN. *(Holding up a joint.)* Wanna go to my room? Smoke a joint?

MEDIUM ALISON. Yes I do.

ALISON. Caption: My newfound queerness was– No. Unable to process this tsunami-like revelation from my father– Tsunami-like??? No.

Bruce smashes down his tool bag in frustration.

Caption: I leapt into my new life with both feet– and I blocked out everything that was happening at home.

Helen is preparing to leave the house for school. Bruce searches through the bag for a tool.

BRUCE. Where the hell are John and Christian???

HELEN. John's at Cosgrove's probably.

BRUCE. Why?

HELEN. *(Taken aback.)* Because… He works there.

ALISON. I should have been paying attention *Caption!* I should have been paying attention.

BRUCE. Since when?

HELEN. He's been working there almost a month.

BRUCE. Oh.

ALISON. And I– *Caption!* I was, I guess I was *mad* at you, Dad.

BRUCE. Well, where's Christian?

HELEN. At Doug's probably. What do you need?

BRUCE. Nothing. Nothing. I'll do it myself.

ALISON. My life had just started to open.

BRUCE. *(Muttering to himself, still searching for the missing tool.)* Dammit! Goddammit!

ALISON. I didn't know, Dad, I had no way of knowing that my beginning would be your end!

> *Helen sees a broken painting.*

HELEN. Oh my god. The Brinley. Oh my god, what happened? Did it fall?

> *He keeps banging around the tool bag, but doesn't answer.*

Bruce, the painting. What happened?

BRUCE. I threw it down the fucking stairs.

HELEN. Why??

BRUCE. I don't // know why!

HELEN. Bruce I don't know // what's–

BRUCE. Because no one fucking helps me around here! Because I can't stand the sound of your hectoring, // shrewish voice, your histrionics, your–

HELEN. You *stop.* You're blaming *me?* After what you've put me through? // I'm on edge every minute. You're so–

BRUCE. Every single person in this town knows what kind of a man I am! *You're* the one with the problem!

HELEN. I have to go to school. I'll be at meetings until late.

> *Helen exits.*

ALISON. I'm drawing. I'm drawing. I'm just drawing. I'm remembering something, that's *all.*

> *SHIFT to Medium Alison and Joan, in their winter coats, with backpacks and a duffle bag, approaching the house.*

MEDIUM ALISON. Oh my god, I don't wanna go in.

JOAN. It's going to be okay.

MEDIUM ALISON. How's it going to be okay? Everything's… Who knows? Who knows? Come on in, let me introduce you to my *gay dad.* It's only three months since I left here! What happened in three months?

> *They enter.*

MEDIUM ALISON. *(Calling out.)* Hello.

> *(To Joan.)*

I don't know where they are.

> *(Calling out.)*

Hey! We're here!

JOAN. *(Looking around, dumbfounded.)* Oh my god.

MEDIUM ALISON. What?

JOAN. You described it, but I had no idea.

MEDIUM ALISON. Why? Oh, yeah, I guess it's–

> *Helen enters.*

HELEN. Oh, you're here.

MEDIUM ALISON. Hi Mom.

HELEN. Is this your friend?

MEDIUM ALISON. Yeah, this is Joan.

JOAN. Thanks for letting me come, Mrs. Bechdel.

HELEN. Very nice to meet you, Joan.

BRUCE. *(Bounding in.)* Hey there you are! Hey! Welcome home! The prodigal returns!!

MEDIUM ALISON. Hey Dad, This is–

BRUCE. Joan!

> *(Shaking her hand.)*

Nice to meet you. Nice to meet you. Listen, I've gotta pick up some three-quarter inch ply from Bittner's before they close. Hey, Kiddo, you wanna go for a drive later?

MEDIUM ALISON. Sure.

> *He leaves.*

So.

HELEN. My goodness, it's lunchtime. Are you girls hungry?

JOAN. I'm okay.

> *(To Medium Alison.)*

You?

MEDIUM ALISON. We're fine.

HELEN. Sure?

MEDIUM ALISON. Yeah, we stopped at a diner on the way. But you should go ahead and eat.

HELEN. No, I'm fine. I might have a glass of wine though. Would either of you like a glass of wine?

MEDIUM ALISON.	**JOAN.**
Uh…	Oh, no thanks, Mrs. Bechdel. *(Beat.)* Maybe you guys would like some time to talk.

	HELEN.
Huh?	Oh.

JOAN. Cuz I actually wouldn't mind laying down a little bit. I'm still pretty wiped out from last week.

MEDIUM ALISON. Okay. Uh–

> *(To Helen.)*

I thought I'd put her in the lilac room?

HELEN. Sure.

MEDIUM ALISON. Upstairs, first room on the right.

JOAN. Great. Come get me whenever.

> *Joan exits.*

HELEN. *(Pouring two glasses of wine.)* You must be tired too.

MEDIUM ALISON. I'm okay.

> *They sit. A beat.*

So.

How've things been here?

HELEN. He bought that old shell of a house out on Route 150. Did he tell you that?

MEDIUM ALISON. Oh yeah, I think he mentioned it in one of his letters. I've been getting two, three, sometimes four letters a week. They're kind of // manic–

HELEN. Years ago he talked about buying it and he looked it over and said it wasn't worth it, it was too far gone and that was back then so I don't know why now that it's even more broken down he's decided he can fix it up. I'm sure he can.

MEDIUM ALISON. Probably.

HELEN. He's out there day and night, like a maniac, not eating, I don't think he's sleeping. Sometimes I walk into a room and he's standing there, not moving, frozen, like a statue.

MEDIUM ALISON. Yeah, I don't know. He's–

HELEN. I'm sick of it. I'm sick of cooking for him and I'm sick of cleaning this museum.

MEDIUM ALISON. It's too much. You've done too much.

HELEN. You know, shortly after we were married we took a drive from Germany where we were living to Paris. He wanted me to meet an Army buddy of his. We had a beautiful drive. And then, just outside of Paris, he just went crazy. Just started screaming at me. Why couldn't I read a simple fucking map? I was a stupid, worthless bitch. I was dumbfounded. I was terrified– it came out of nowhere as far as I knew. Of course, I learned later that this man had been your father's lover.

MEDIUM ALISON. I don't know how you've done it.

HELEN.

Welcome to our house on Maple Avenue
See how we polish and we shine
We rearrange and realign
Everything is balanced and…and…
Days and days and days, that's how it happens
Days and days and days
made of lunches and car rides and shirts and socks

HELEN. *(cont.)*

> *and grades and piano and no one clocks*
> *the day you disappear*
> *Days and days and days, that's how it happens*
> *Days and days and days*
> *made of posing and bragging and fits of rage*
> *and boys, my god, some of them underage*
> *And oh how did it all happen here?*
>
> *There was a time your father swept me off my feet with words*
> *We read books, strolled through Munich at night,*
> *drank beer with friends, discussed the places we would go*
> *And he said I understood how the world made him ache*
> *But no*
> *But no*
>
> *That's how it happens*
> *Days made of bargains I made because I thought as a wife*
> *I was meant to and now my life is shattered and laid bare*
> *Days and days and days and days and days and days and days*
>
> *Welcome to our house on Maple Avenue*
> *See how we polish and we shine*
> *We rearrange and realign*
> *Everything is balanced and serene*
> *Like chaos never happens if it's never seen*
>
> *Don't you come back here*
> *I didn't raise you*
> *to give away your days*
> *like me*

SHIFT to Bruce and Joan at the piano.

BRUCE.

> *That's how Mavis and Pearl and Carol*
> *In fancy hats and parasols*
> *Ended up together inside that barrel*
> *Tumbling down Niagara Falls!*
> *Ba da ba da ba*
> *Ba da ba da ba*
> *Ba da ba da ba!*
> And we sang it for the dean's wife!

JOAN. No!

BRUCE. Oh yes.

JOAN. What happened???

BRUCE. The crowd went wild!

JOAN. I can't believe you did that!

Medium Alison enters.

BRUCE. Listen, as far as we knew we were about to be expelled anyway, so we thought why not stick it to the man on our way out!

MEDIUM ALISON. Oh god, this story?

JOAN. You didn't tell me your dad was a troublemaker.

MEDIUM ALISON. Has he got you polishing silver??

JOAN. I don't know what to say. He made it sound like a great idea.

BRUCE. I charmed her into it.

JOAN. He charmed me into it.

BRUCE. *(Playing the bottom part of "Heart and Soul.")* Hey Al, come play this one with your old dad.

Medium Alison is also now having a good time.

MEDIUM ALISON. No. Dad!

BRUCE. *(To Joan.)* Have you heard her play?

JOAN. I have not.

BRUCE. Aha! Well, she learned everything she knows from me. Keep that in mind. Come on!

MEDIUM ALISON. Dad!

BRUCE. Come on.

Heart and soul–

BRUCE & MEDIUM ALISON. *(With gusto.)*

Jean Stafford must have loved Robert Lowell
because he treated her badly
They took the same romantic path
as Hughes and Plath

MEDIUM ALISON. *(Cutting the song off, laughing.)* Enough!

JOAN. You wrote that?

BRUCE. It was a collaboration.

ALISON. There's a different version of this visit, Dad, where it's all alright, where everything turns out alright.

> *Bruce continues to play on the piano. More laughter.*

JOAN. I'm gonna go help your mom with dinner.

> *She exits, leaving Medium Alison and Bruce alone together. Bruce continues to tinker on the piano.*

BRUCE. Joan's a great gal.

MEDIUM ALISON. Yeah?

BRUCE. Oh yeah. Quick. Bright.

MEDIUM ALISON. Yeah, she is. Yeah.

> *Beat.*

Hey, Dad?

BRUCE. Yeah?

MEDIUM ALISON. I've been wondering…

BRUCE. Yeah?

MEDIUM ALISON. I was just wondering…if you knew what you were doing when you gave me that Colette book.

> *Bruce continues tinkering on the piano. Then, finally, shrugs it off, amiably:*

BRUCE. I don't know.

> *He continues his idle playing for a beat, then gets up and grabs his jacket.*

You ready to go for that drive?

Kiddo?

> *His attention shifts seamlessly from Medium Alison to adult Alison.*

Alison?

> *She is taken aback.*

You ready?

A beat. Then:

ALISON. Yes.

BRUCE. *(Flipping his car keys.)* Wanna drive?

ALISON. No, that's okay. You can drive.

> *She follows him into the car. She's not remembering this, she's living it again. They drive.*

BRUCE. So…

> *(He gathers his nerve.)*

It's, uh… It's, uh…

> *(Small nervous chuckle. He tries again.)*

You, uh…

> *(Can't do it.)*

That too much air?

ALISON. Um-mm.

> *They drive in painful silence. She looks out the window, her eyes following the telephone wires.*

Telephone wire
run and run
Telephone wire
sun down on the creek
Partly frozen, partly flowing,
must be windy, trees are bending,
Junction 50,
field needs mowing
Feels like the
car is floating

Say something, talk to him
Say something, anything
At the light
at the light
at the light
at the light

ALISON. *(cont.)*

> *At the light*
> *at the light*
> *at the light*
> *at the light*
> *Like, you could say,*
> *So how does it feel to know that you and I are both–*

BRUCE. Hey

ALISON. Yeah?

BRUCE.

> *Where'd'ya wanna go?*

ALISON.

> *Oh. I don't know.*

BRUCE.

> *I know a bar*
> *It's kind of hidden away*
> *Seedy club*
> *for folks like, you know…*
> *Could be fun*

ALISON.

> *But Dad*
> *I'm not twenty-one*

BRUCE. Oh yeah. Right.

ALISON.

> *Telephone wire*
> *Long black line*
> *Telephone wire*
> *Finely threaded sky*
> *There's the pond where I went wading,*
> *there's the sign for Sugar Valley,*
> *on the mountain light is fading*
> *I go back to school tomorrow*
>
> *Say something, talk to him*
> *Say something, anything*
>
> *At the light*
> *at the light*

at the light
at the light

At the light
at the light
at the light
at the light
Doesn't matter what you say
Just make the fear in his eyes go away

BRUCE.

There was a boy
In college
My first year there
Norris Jones
He had black wavy hair

Huh.

Norris Jones
Where is he now?

Fourteen years old
In Swensen's barn
It was cold
Lots of boys messed around, you know
For them, it was a game they outgrew
But I always knew

ALISON.

Dad, me too!
Since, like five, I guess
I preferred to wear boys shirts and pants
I felt absurd in a dress
I really tried to deny my feelings for girls
But I was like you
Dad, me too

BRUCE.

Huh.

Norris Jones

ALISON. Dad?

BRUCE.

Norris Jones

ALISON. Dad?

BRUCE. Did I mention I've taken on a new project?

That old house out on Route 150!

You've seen it, Al. It's been sitting empty out there for forty, fifty years at least.

ALISON.

Telephone wire

Stop! Too fast!

Telephone wire

Make this not the past, this car ride!

This is where it has to happen

There must be some other chances

There's a moment I'm forgetting where you tell me you see me

Say something, talk to me!

Say something, anything!

At the light!

At the light!

This can't be our last–

BRUCE. That was fun.

> **They're home.**

It's earlier than I thought.

> **He gets out of the car.**

Comin' in?

ALISON. *(Still in the car.)*

Telephone wire

That was our last night

> **Alison tries to pull herself together the way she always has, by working.**

This, um… What is this? Table in the living room with– jack in the pulpit. Oh. Oh. That's, uh, I was going to draw that // in this panel.

> **The table goes away. Bruce enters.**

BRUCE. Dear Al, It was great to have you home.

ALISON. What was I…?

> **She looks for something else to draw.**

What's this?

BRUCE. I've been flying high ever since you were here.

ALISON. This. I can draw this draw this in the…

> *The object disappears.*

Oh.

> *She looks for something else to draw.*

BRUCE. Dear Al

ALISON. This is good. This is good. I could… I could…

> *The object disappears. Alison wheels around to face her father.*

BRUCE.	ALISON.
I'll admit I'm somewhat envious of the 'new' freedom that appears on campuses today.	
	(Fierce.)
Dear Al, Did you receive that Winogrand article I was telling you about?	What did it feel like to step in front of a truck, Dad? What did it feel like to see it coming right at you and not move? And just let it hit you? Why?
You should have gotten it by now.	
Do you know I was never even in New York until I was about twenty?	Was it because of me? Did it have *nothing* to do with me? *What Happened?*
Dear Al, I just re-read *Araby*. That could have been me– I was rather sensitive when I was little, you know–	
Dear Al, I've been working like mad on that house I told you about. Can't think about much else. Can't sleep–	
Dear Al–	

BRUCE.

> *I fucking love beginnings*
> *Flying high*
> *Hard to know where to start*
> *It's all so fast I'm trying not to spin*
> *I guess I'm older*
> *And it's harder when you're older to begin*
> *Peeling plaster, sagging roof,*
> *two missing stairs, a buckled wall*
> *I'm fired up to do this*
> *But on my own it all…*
>
> *So much damage, broken windows,*
> *pipes are shit, crap veneer*
> *It's hours later, Jesus, I'm still standing here*
> *Still standing here*
>
> *But when the sunlight hits the parlor wall*
> *at certain times of day*
> *I see how fine this house could be*
> *I see it so damn clear*
> *What's the matter? Why am I standing here?*
>
> *Bad foundation, twisting floorboards,*
> *shoddy pipes, a gaping hole*
> *It's a lot, it's a lot to keep under control*
> *Something cracking, something rotting,*
> *piles of ruin and debris,*
> *killing me! crushing me! pushing me!*
>
> *But when the sunlight hits the parlor wall*
> *at certain times of day*
> *I see how fine this house could be*
> *I see it so damn clear*
> *What's the matter? Why am I standing here?*
>
> *Dear Al, I'm scared.*
> *I had a life I thought I understood.*
> *I took it and I squeezed out every bit of life I could.*
> *But the edges of the world that held me up have gone away*
> *and I'm falling into nothingness*
> *or flying into something so sublime*

and I'm a man I don't know
Who am I now? Where do I go?
I can't go back
I can't find my way through
I might still break a heart or two
But when the sunlight hits the parlor wall
at certain times of day
I see how fine this house could be
I see it so damn clear
Oh my God!
Why am I standing here?

> **Glare of headlights. Unbearable, deafening sound of a blaring car horn.**

> **And then he's gone.**

> **Alison, shattered, reflexively returns to her drawing table, to her work.**

ALISON. Caption.

Caption.

Caption.

Caption. Caption.

> **She realizes the obvious.**

I'm the only one here.

> **She drops her pen. She picks up a stack of useless drawings.**

This is what I have of you:

> *(Paging through them.)*

You ordering me to sweep and dust the parlor.
You steaming off the wallpaper.
You in front of a classroom of bored students.
Digging up a dogwood tree.
You working on the house, smelling like sawdust
and sweat and designer cologne.
You calling me at college to tell me how I'm
supposed to feel about Faulkner or Hemingway.

The next one blindsides her.

ALISON. *(cont.)* You...standing on the shoulder of Route 150
   bracing yourself against the pulse of the
   trucks rushing past.

> *And the next one...is of the one thing she's ever
> really wanted from him.*

You...*succumbing* to a rare moment of physical
contact with me.

> *She grabs her pen and draws:*

Daddy (comma) hey Daddy
come here okay (question mark)
I need // you

> *Small Alison appears.*

SMALL ALISON.

   Daddy, hey, Daddy, come here, okay, I need you.

> *Medium Alison appears.*

MEDIUM ALISON.

   At the light
   at the light
   at the light
   at the light

ALISON.

   What are you doing (question mark)
   I said come here
   You need //to do what I tell you to do

SMALL ALISON.

   What are you doing?
   I said come here!
   You need to do what I tell you to do.

SMALL ALISON.   MEDIUM ALISON.

   Listen to me. Daddy!

   Come here, hey right here,   *At the light*
   right now, you're making me
        mad.

SMALL ALISON. *(cont.)*   **MEDIUM ALISON.** *(cont.)*
   Listen to me.   *How does it feel to know –*
   Listen to me.
   Listen to me.
   I wanna play airplane

MEDIUM ALISON.
   That you and I–

SMALL ALISON.
   I wanna play airplane

MEDIUM ALISON.
   That you and I–

SMALL ALISON.
   I wanna play airplane

ALISON.
   I wanna put my arms out and fly

MEDIUM ALISON.
   I was like you

SMALL ALISON. Like the Red Baron in his Sopwith Camel!
   No, wait-
   Like Superman

ALISON.
   up in the sky

MEDIUM ALISON.
   Say something

ALISON.
   'Til I can see all of Pennsylvania

MEDIUM.
   Say something

SMALL ALISON.
   Put your feet here like this, Daddy, do what I say

ALISON. *(Looking at a drawing.)*
   There you are, Dad.

SMALL ALISON.

Take my hands, give me yours
Bend your knees, not that way

When I say go, you start
pushing me up, okay?

ALISON.

Don't let go yet

SMALL ALISON.

Okay, higher
just a little

ALISON.

And now I'm flying away

MEDIUM ALISON.

Look at me fly away

SMALL ALISON.

–in my wristband and cape

THREE ALISONS.

Fly

SMALL ALISON.

–up so high
Our house is over there, and there's our car
The Fun Home, I see it!
I'm up so far

SMALL ALISON.

Daddy, there's your school!
And there's Grandma's house!
There's Uncle Pete's farm!

I can see all of
Pennsylvania

ALISON.

I can see all of Pennsylvania

SMALL ALISON.

I can see all of Pennsylvania

THREE ALISONS.

Fly away

ALISON.

There you are

MEDIUM ALISON.

Okay
Okay

MEDIUM ALISON.

So far

Pennsylvania

SMALL ALISON.

This is the best game. Up in the air!

ALISON.

A picture of my father

SMALL ALISON.

And I don't even care that it pushes my stomach in.

ALISON.

Made of little marks

SMALL ALISON.	ALISON.	MEDIUM ALISON
Fly		
	Beautiful	*Fly*
up so high		
Fly	*Fly*	*Fly*
up so high		
Fly	*Fly*	*Fly*
up so high		*Fly*

SMALL ALISON.

I can see all of Pennsylvania

ALISON. Caption: Every so often there was a rare moment of perfect balance when I soared above him.

End

CPSIA information can be obtained
at www.ICGtesting.com
Printed in the USA
BVHW05s0451290418
514745BV00017B/670/P